Lincoln *and* His Boys

Lincoln *and* His Boys

Rosemary Wells
illustrated by P. J. Lynch

CANDLEWICK PRESS

For Amy
and with thanks to Catherine Clinton—R.W.

For David and Penelope
with special thanks to Luke, Ben, and Aidan—P.J.L.

Text copyright © 2009 by Rosemary Wells

Illustrations copyright © 2009 by P.J. Lynch

First edition 2009

Library of Congress Cataloging-in-Publication Data

Wells, Rosemary.

Lincoln and his boys / Rosemary Wells ; illustrated by P.J. Lynch. — 1st ed.

p. cm.

Summary: Brothers Willie and Taddie share stories about their father,
Abraham Lincoln, from 1859 to 1865.

ISBN 978-0-7636-3723-1

1. Lincoln, Abraham, 1809–1865—Juvenile fiction. [1. Lincoln, Abraham, 1809–1865—Fiction.
2. Lincoln, William Wallace, 1850–1862—Fiction. 3. Lincoln, Thomas, 1853–1871—Fiction.
4. Children of presidents—Fiction.] I. Lynch, P.J., ill. II. Title.

PZ7.W46843 Fat 2009

[Fic]—dc22   2008021418

2 4 6 8 10 9 7 5 3 1

Printed in the United States of America

This book was typeset in Adobe Jenson.

The illustrations were done in oil.

Candlewick Press

99 Dover Street

Somerville, Massachusetts 02144

visit us at www.candlewick.com

Willie
— 1859 —

Every evening my brother Tad and I run over to Father's office on the corner of Adams Street. We huck handfuls of pebbles up at the windowpanes so Father knows we are coming. Tad is smaller than I am, but he can throw the pebbles harder and make more noise.

Mr. Herndon, Father's law partner, likes things neat and quiet. He says we act like little wild orangutans, which is true. But Father doesn't ever scold us for what we do. If Mr. Herndon gets that look on his face and shakes his finger at us, Father laughs. Tad makes most of the trouble. I never squirt ink or ruin briefs. Mostly I stack the big old law books and make pyramids out of them and then knock them all down. It's our job, says Mama, to pull Father out of his office and get him home for supper on time, so that's what we do after the sun goes down.

On the walk home to our house on Jackson and Eighth, Father and Tad and I always stop and talk to neighbors and dogs, which makes us late. Then we run into the house and Father puts his arms around Mama and waltzes her around the room until she smiles and comes out of her fretfulness about our being late for supper.

When we sit at table, Mama makes dead sure we have good manners. We are not allowed resting on elbows. Sometimes she chides Father for wearing shirtsleeves around the house and not putting on his coat. He puts on his coat to make her happy. Then he puts his hand over his smile and declares the coat has

just taken flight like an eagle and come to rest on the back of his chair.

We chew with mouths closed and don't slurp our soup. Tad has trouble eating. He was born with a hole in the roof of his mouth and has to have all his food cut up for him. His manners are not as good as mine, but they are on the way up.

Tonight at supper, when Tad pulled my hair, Mama said, "Taddie darling, who knows where we'll be a year from now? It might be in the finest palaces of Paris, France! They don't let little boys with no table manners eat in the dining rooms in the palaces!"

Immediately I wonder why Mama says this about palaces in France. It might could mean she is planning an escape from Springfield to a fancier place. Long ago Father was a congressman in Washington. Does this mean Father is redding up for another election? Willie and I discuss it in bed.

"Mama ordered a new black suit for Papa-day," says Taddie from his pillow. "She sent money in the letter. Two pair of trousers."

"How do you know?" I ask.

"She told me," Taddie answers. "She let me mail the letter to Mr. Steinway, the tailor in Chicago. That's how. I said to Mama, 'What's this letter for, Mama?' and she tried to get me to read the address and I couldn't. But then she said it's to Mr. Steinway's tailor shop on Dearborn Avenue in Chicago. It's for a new suit."

"What do you think the new suit means, Tad?" I ask.

Tad doesn't hesitate. "Papa-day's gonna turn around and re-whup Mr. Douglas." Taddie always says *Papa-day*; it's his way of saying *Papa dear*. Taddie's cleft palate gives him lots of lispy speech trouble.

Sometimes I have to translate what he says to people outside the family. A lot of people think Taddie is slow, but he doesn't miss a thing. He's as smart as a snake. When the time is right, I'll ask Father if indeed he's working up to another scrap with Mr. Douglas. Mr. Douglas beat Father in the Senate election in '58. We did not like that one bit, since Mr. Douglas told lies about Father during their debates.

It is decided that I, Willie, have good enough manners that I may visit Chicago with Father when he goes to the courthouse there in early June. I am more excited than I have ever been in my nine years on earth.

On June 2nd, the morning of our trip, Mama parts my hair with her ivory comb. She slicks it down both sides with water. It stays in place until the station. Then she kisses the top of my head when the train comes down the tracks. I let go her hand and change it for Father's. Her hand is no bigger than a plump little sparrow. His hand is hard and brown and the span of my whole arm.

Father scoops up my small bag and his large one. A strand of Mama's black hair has come loose. It blows in her face until she tucks it back into its bun. She waves to us until I know it hurts her arm. Her eyes are shaded with her other hand, and she is squinting under the sun until she can't see us or the train anymore.

Now I have Father all to myself. "This is a superior train, Pa," I tell him proudly because it is my first train. Father says that it's a pretty tinky railway compared to others in Pennsylvania and New York.

It takes all of a day to get to Chicago. Father and I walk to the Tremont Hotel. I never did imagine so many people or so much noise all in one place.

"Willie, you look like the preacher on his first day in heaven," Father says to me. "Surprised to see that so many other people got there too!"

People say about Father that he's pine tall. This is due to his double-long legs. In the way that tall people do, Father tips sideways to hold my hand.

In the Tremont Hotel lobby is a whole forest of trees set in porcelain tubs. I ask what their strange long leaves are. Father says they are palms. "The palm has a frond, not a leaf," he explains. "*F-r-o-n-d*. Frond."

I spell it back to him and he is pleased.

Then there is strange music. It is not fiddle. It is not piano or horn.

"What is it, Pa? What is that little popping music?" I ask him.

"It's a harp," says Father.

So I say, "That lady playing it must be an angel. Only angels play harps!"

Father agrees that she must be an angel. He tells me, "Close your mouth, son, and don't forget to blink your eyes once in a while!"

Suddenly a whole bunch of men come up and talk to Father. A year ago, when he was running against Mr. Douglas, these same sort of men were always circling Father and doing the same important-sounding talk. Father loves to talk back. It's because he is a lawyer, and Mama says lawyers are paid a dollar a minute to chatter away like monkeys in the trees.

One of the men comes over and claps me on the back. His shirt is moon white, his fingernails clean and shined up like a woman's.

I must be quiet and wait until they stop talking.

If spoken to, I must answer with a straight-shooter look in my eyes, Father tells me. "That's the key to it. Look them spang in the eye and speak up. Then they won't treat you like a squirt," he says.

I watch Father talk to these spiffed-up men with soft hands. He makes them listen and makes them laugh. He's easy with them. It's Mama who taught him just how to be easy with rich men. Mama comes from Kentucky people who own a fine amount of land. They drink out of pure crystal glasses and ride fancy horses. Mama knows about how to be rich like these men. She's proud of it.

We sit down to supper in the hotel dining room. It looks sheerly like the royal banquet hall in *King Arthur and the Knights of the Round Table.*

Father says to me, "I am going to shoot the breeze with you, Will, about a very grown-up set of things." He picks a piece of bread out of the basket that the waiter brings us and takes a bite of it. "I can talk to you, Scout, better than to your big brother."

Bob Lincoln is my big brother. He is away in the East at preparatory school. He'd be at Harvard but he failed his exams and must try again. Father and Bob haven't ever been close friends like Father and me. They get under each other's skins.

I ask Father, "Pa, is it those fancy duded-up men? Do they want you to run in another election?"

"You are sharp as a new tack, Scout," he says. He opens his menu and orders for both of us to the waiter, who writes it down on a pad.

I cannot eat my bread because my mouth goes a little dry. "They want you to leave home again and travel all over the place? Like you did when you were running against Mr. Douglas?" I ask.

"I will have to travel even as far as New York and Massachusetts and Maine, son. That's a far piece! You must take care of your Mama now that Bobby's not home."

"Taddie and me, we hate being home without you, Pa," I say. "Mama is always fretful when you're not there. She treads back and forth in the bedroom and makes the floor squeak."

"I know it. There's not a thing I can do about it."

"Will you be senator this time, Pa?" I ask.

"President, son."

"President of the whole United States?" I say. I don't think I heard him right.

He looks in my eyes. He says, "Will, it's a derby race, and I've got a plow horse's chance. But if somebody doesn't shake these Southern blockheads in Washington by the ears, we'll be living in a different country next year. Slavery's going to split America the way an ax cuts an apple."

All of the last year, Father and Mr. Douglas

debated up and down the state of Illinois. Mr. Douglas was for slavery being allowed in every state. Father was against it. Mr. Douglas won the election, but Father got to be famous all the way to Boston and New York for his speeches.

He has ordered us oysters, roast quail, steak royale, and sherbet Jenny Lind. We eat every bite.

"Who is Jenny Lind?" I want to know.

"She is the best lady singer in the world," says Father. "That is why they named an ice cream for her. Tomorrow night we will go and hear her at McVicker's Theatre."

Father loves entertainments. When he was a boy, he had no entertainments ever. Brother Bob told Tad and me that when Father was a boy, he lived in a poky little shack in the middle of the wild forest. Father's own pappy was a sometime drunk, says

Brother Bob. Mostly out of work. He beat Father for reading too many books.

Bob told me and Taddie in secret that Father disliked his own pappy so much he wouldn't so much as visit the old man on his deathbed or raise a tombstone over his grave. This is not entirely true, Mama said when she heard the story. Father tried a deathbed visit the year before, but his pappy stayed alive. However it is, we don't ever see any kin from the Lincoln side, only Mama's side. Mama's people, the Todds, live in Lexington, and my uncle Ninian gives me the piece of mint out of his mint julep and I suck the sugar off it and eat the lemon peel.

In the morning, we go to the Cook County Courthouse. Father puts on his glasses and commences two hours of lawyer work. I sit in a window seat and read everything in the *Chicago Tribune*.

Across the room, Father winks at me. He's talking to heavy-suited other lawyers who smoke cigars and chew big wads of tobacco. They spit squirts of brown tobacco juice into the metal cuspidors around the corners of the room. I hate that. So does Father.

Somewhere a noon whistle blows. Father folds up his glasses and squirrels them away in a breast pocket. We are suddenly free.

We hop on the Dearborn Street horse trolley. The first stop is Mr. Steinway. All Father's suits are black. Mama says you don't want to trust a man who wears blue suits or brown suits, because they look cheap. Mama sees to it that Father wears respectable clothes and cravats. She has to, to keep him up with the other biggity lawyers.

"You, sir, are the longest man in Illinois," says Mr. Steinway, his mouth full of pins.

I tell Father, "Pa, Taddie knew you were going to run again the minute Mama ordered up that suit."

"He reads the signs well, Scout," says Father.

"Pa, will you have to run against Senator Douglas again?"

"Most likely," answers Father. He holds out his arms for Mr. Steinway to measure.

"I don't like Senator Douglas," I tell him. "The boys at school won't let me forget he skunked you in the election. How did such a wormy little man skunk you, Pa?"

"Senator Douglas is not a wormy little man," says Father.

"Brother Bob says he is," I tell him.

Mr. Steinway makes marks along the lines of the lapels and down the back of the coat sleeves.

Father doesn't answer. Sometimes he likes to

visit inside himself and his eyes go away to a place that only he is allowed to see.

At last he says, "There are a hundred reasons why things happen, Willie. Those reasons fan out like circles around a stone thrown into a pond. The stone in the center of those reason rings is called truth. Truth is the very hardest thing on earth to see clear."

"What is the truth?" I ask him.

Father smiles that big grin that changes his whole face, and his eyes come back to me. "Next year I will skunk Senator Douglas!"

"How are you going to do it?" I want to know.

Father's left eyelid closes and he does not answer me when or how. "We will get your mother a pair of kid gloves for her birthday," he tells me, and his hand strays to my hair and he messes it up.

***

Palmer's Circus of Dry Good Dreams is a thousand times as big as the general store in Springfield. The glove lady places a rainbow of kid gloves on the high counter for us to study. Father braces me up to see.

"Red," I say, "because Mama's fancy shoes are red."

"Blue," says Father. "Because forget-me-nots are her favorite."

We cannot decide. So we go over to belt buckles and get a nice steel one to send to Bob at school. We get socks for Taddie and caramels for me and Taddie. Then we go back to the gloves. We still can't agree, red or blue, and so we buy both colors.

"We will go to McVicker's now and purchase two tickets for Jenny Lind," says Father.

"Pa, what will Miss Jenny Lind sing tonight?" I ask.

"Probably songs in German and Italian," answers my father.

"Will I like that, Pa?"

"Your mother made me swear on a stack of Bibles I would take you to hear Miss Jenny Lind for your edification, son."

"I heard her say it, Pa. She said she doesn't want me growing up to be a prairie tick like other people she was not going to name."

"Exactly so, son. Your mother is completely right. I am a prairie tick," says Father.

"Pa, the newspaper had a notice that the Chinese acrobats and jugglers are in town. They are at Metropolitan Hall."

We see both shows.

On the train home the next morning, I sit back and close my eyes. I dream of the Chinese acrobats.

Genies in red silk twirl on silver balls. Wizards in gold silk fly through the air, filling my sleepy mind.

Father reads a book. When he reads, he reads aloud. He makes pencil notes on the pages. I watch his lips form the words. The train is bumpy as horseback. Sometimes his glasses fall off his nose.

"What is that, Pa?" I ask.

"It's a play by Shakespeare called *Julius Caesar*," Father answers. He looks in my face and explains, "I have no proper schooling, son, not a nickel more than nine months altogether. Next year there will be a squad of patroons running against me. They all have Harvard educations and were born in silk pajamas. Your pa does not want to sound like a prairie tick alongside 'em on the podium. Shakespeare is a tonic for the mind. It plates the tongue with silver."

We head into Springfield. "Look, Pa! Mama is

on the platform waiting!" I shout. "She has brought Taddie to meet us!"

Father puts away his Shakespeare. "Always," he says, "she is afraid of the angel of darkness when we are not with her."

I know about that angel of darkness. It came and brushed over Mama when my least brother, Eddie, died of fever. He was only three. Ever since Eddie, Mama has been fearful.

I say to Father, "But in the hotel we saw a good angel playing the harp, didn't we, Pa?"

"We will tell her," says Father.

"And we will give her the gloves now and not wait for her birthday!" I say because I see the worry frown above Mama's eyes through the window of the train.

Then Father lifts me up. He puts his whole face

into my hair because he loves to smell it. Then the train stops and we alight into the sun.

Willie *and* Tad
— 1861 —

Father has been elected president, but some busybody little girl writes him a letter and says he'd look much snappier in whiskers, so he is growing a beard on his chin, no mustache. "It is a good time to grow whiskers," he says. "We will have twelve days on this train before we get to Washington. By the time I wave to all the people in Washington, D.C., they will never know I started out the trip clean-shaven."

Some nights we sleep on the train. Some nights we get off and stay at a hotel. Each day the beard gets a little thicker. Father rehearses his speech that he will give on the first day he is president. He writes and rewrites and then he reads it out loud and crosses out some and begins again.

At one hotel Father gave the speech in a satchel to Bob for safekeeping. But Bob found a bunch of young people and went out for brandy fizzes. He lost Father's inauguration speech, the only copy. I have never seen Father so angry, but it turned up in the hotel baggage room after a two-hour search.

The train goes slowly and stops at every little town in Indiana and Ohio. Tad asks me to read out the names of the stations and I do. Lebanon, Cadiz Junction, Ashtabula. Taddie says the town names after me.

At each stop the train fills with men and then

empties of some of them farther along the line. Some of them are in uniform, some in suits. They want to talk to Father all the time.

People in the towns come out to see Father and hear his voice. Sometimes they get close enough to the train to stare in the window of our car.

"Who are they?" I want to know.

"Farmers, mostly," says Father. "Look at their boots. You can tell a farmer from a drover because one's got muddy brogans and the other's got rider's boots. Then there's the shopkeepers. Clean leather shoes on them. Kits, cats, sacks, and wives. They need to see the face of the man they elected president. Otherwise I am just an engraving in the newspaper."

Somewhere in east Ohio a man mounts the platform and comes shyly to our window with a tin box in his arms. He is covered in flour as if with snow. Out of the tin box he removes two muffins, wrapped in heavy napkins, still hot from the oven. They drip butter. He holds them out to me and Taddie. I thank the baker and smile.

The baker cannot take his eyes off us. He says, "I will tell my children that I fed my muffins to President Lincoln's sons. Someday they will tell their children about it, and their children after that. Off into time ever after! Can you imagine!"

"Eat your muffin, Taddie," I say. But Taddie does not eat his muffin. He holds it in his hand, letting the butter drip onto the track below us. I watch him. His

eyes are glued to something at the other side of the wall. After a few minutes, a little girl dressed in rags strolls up to the train window. Her face is covered with sores. Taddie gives her his muffin. He grins at her, and she eats it with her eyes closed as if she had never eaten anything so good in her life.

"She had the pox," says Taddie when we begin rolling again.

The people want to see Mama and so she is in her best dress, which she has just bought in Indianapolis. They want to see us, me and Taddie, but Taddie won't do it. He lies on the floor of our train car, rips off his cravat, and kicks his feet and says, "When are we going to get there? I want to go outside and run around!" until Bob says, "Taddie, shut up whining! It doesn't make the train go any faster."

Mama says, "Don't say 'shut up' to your brother, Bobby. It's common talk."

I don't think Bob cares, because he is on his way to Harvard College and that's where his whole mind is.

Mama takes Tad on her lap and gives him sugared tea and a slice of apple we got on the platform from the last station. They are winter-softened Macouns from somebody's cold cellar. Mama sings with Tad and lets him go through every item in her handbag.

Between stops, Father gets down on the floor with us. Dust soils the knees of his new president's suit. He doesn't mind. He plays horse with me and Tad until he says his spine is going to give out. Then the brakes squeal and the train shudders to another stop.

Father tries to slide me off his back. "People are waiting," he says. "They want me to tell them I will make the war clouds go away."

"What are war clouds, Pa?" I ask astride his back, holding on to his ears.

"Gathering to the south," says Father, pointing to the right side of the train. I see no clouds. Only bright March sun.

Father goes on, "Willie, the South wants to shear its states off from the rest of the country. They have their own president, Jefferson Davis, a four-flusher if there ever was one. They are determined to split the country across the middle — half slave, half free — and they'll start a war to do it. It's my job not to let them do it."

"How are you going to not let them?" I ask.

He stands up, brushing off the knees of his trousers. He takes Tad from Mama and looks out the window with me, curling his arm around my side. His eye closes as it does sometimes, and there is no answer, I think because he doesn't quite know.

Nothing about war clouds is real until Harrisburg, Pennsylvania, and then danger is on us. We are at the Jones Hotel with Governor Curtin. I am very bored and yawny because the day has been full of more speeches and hours of Tad and me sitting up properly in our best suits not fiddling around or kicking.

Suddenly Father comes up to us at the children's supper in the hotel dining room. We are served vegetable soup, and Taddie takes all the peas out and puts them on the nice linen cloth. Father is wearing someone else's eyeglasses, a low-crown hat, and a light gray coat.

"Pa, why are you dressed that way?" I ask.

"Just a lot of shicoonery, Scout," he says. "Mr. Pinkerton is dressing me like a haberdasher and putting me on a fast train to Washington."

"But why, Pa?" I ask. "Who is Mr. Pinkerton?"

"See you tomorrow, Scout!" is his answer.

Taddie grabs Father by the lapels of his strange gray coat until Father takes Tad's hands and places them back on the tablecloth. "Eat every single one of those peas, son!" he says, spooning them up and putting them back in Tad's soup. He winks and then is gone.

We board the train—Mama, Taddie, Bob, and me. Mama says nothing, but her mouth is a tight line of worry.

Later, when we are rumbling through Pennsylvania, Bob comes over to my bunk. "Mr. Pinkerton," Bob whispers, "is a detective from

Chicago with a passel of hired police to protect Father."

"But what happened?" I want to know.

"Some Copperheads in Baltimore threatened Pa's life, Will. That's what."

"Who are Copperheads?" I want to know.

Bob answers, "The Copperheads are border staters. They've got rebel hearts. They hate real hard, and they wanted to kill Pa because he will stand against the slave states."

I have no idea what a border state is. I suppose they can't decide if they are North or South. Our train is heading to Baltimore, Maryland. A huge tangle of copperhead moccasin snakes appears in my mind. I tell myself to lie, hands at sides, stiff as a board. I tell myself if I don't move a muscle all night long, then Father will be safe from Copperheads.

"You wait, Willie," Bob goes on. "Pa's going to be

swallowed up by the war because it's coming soon."
He tells me he wants to enlist in the army instead of
going to Harvard but Mama won't hear of it. Then
he snugs my blanket under my chin and turns out the
blinky little gas lamp over my bed.

In the morning, Mama is all rustle and bustle,
and by that I know that Father is not dead.

There is a comet in the sky over Washington city. Its
tail is to the north and its head to the south.
Everyone says the comet means that the North will
strike an arrow into the heart of the rebel states. Just
before supper, I see Father at his new desk in the
president's office, one foot propped up on an open
drawer. Mr. Nicolay and Mr. Hay, Father's private
secretaries, have gone home for the day. Father is
staring out at the war comet.

I whisper to Taddie. "He's coming up for air.

Mr. Nicolay says over a hundred people came to see him today."

"I hate all those people," says Taddie.

"You can't say *hate*, Taddie. It's wrong."

"I hate them anyway," says Taddie.

I give Tad a little kick in the back of his shoe. He knows he is not supposed to say *hate*, because it is uncharitable talk. But if the truth were told, I would have to say I hate the hundreds of visitors too, because they wander around the President's House, all these unknown people, and want favors from Father. No one stops them. They clip off little pieces of the rugs and other things for souvenirs. They line up in the halls and fight about who's first in line. Now that Father is president, they want him to give them jobs and money and letters written on their behalf. They eat up Father's time, and it's hard to get to play with him the way we used to. So sometimes we have to drag Father out of meetings. He is never too unhappy about it.

Tonight he hears Tad and me scuffling. He turns and sees us. His face lights up and he says, "Who's that foolishing in the hall?"

"It's us, Pa!" I say. He sits down on a couch and pulls me into his lap. Tad comes along.

"How do you like this big old president's mansion?" Father asks. Father lifts Taddie up and sits him on the table next to us. Taddie bangs his feet, and Father quiets him with a hand on his ankles.

"We love it, Papa-day," says Tad.

"Mama says she's turned up some playmates for you. The Taft boys?"

"Holly and Bud. They come with their sister. She's supposed to mind us, but we don't let her."

"Holly and Bud are good codgers?" asks Father.

"We are as four brothers now," I answer him.

Then Father goes into his office and we clomp after him. He points out the window to the sky. "Look at that!" he says. "Some little star got loose in the sky!"

"It's the war comet," I say to Father.

"So they say," he answers.

"Do you really think it's a war comet, that it's true, Pa?"

"Somewhere in the South some fool will light a fuse," he says, "and the war will begin. It's only a matter of days. If the comet is here to announce that, then the comet speaks the truth."

"Will we win the war, Pa?" I ask.

He smiles. "If I can get us the services of Colonel Robert E. Lee, best man in the army, then we stand a fair chance of whippin' the rebels," he says.

"We'll help, Pa!" I say. "We have made a fort on the roof, me and Tad and Holly and Bud. We have cannons, swords, and muskets that we found in the attic. We have everything we need except fire. Pa, can we light a campfire up there?" I ask. "Please, just a little one?"

"The answer is no," says Father. "It is a real and big no, Willie. The whole President's House could go up like a box of matches. Now, swear you won't do it, Willie."

I put my hand under his vest on his shirt over his heart until I feel it beating against my palm. "I swear no fire, Pa," I say. I take Taddie's hand and make him swear the same oath.

We have been busy, Tad and me, Holly and Bud. The President's House has as many rooms as a good-size hotel. The green room has disgusting moldy sofas and chairs. We bounce on them, but clouds of dust and mold come up and make us sneeze. Some rooms are filled with boring old statues and paintings in flaking gold frames. But there are secret attics upstairs above our living rooms. There are basement storerooms downstairs near the kitchen. In them Tad and me, Bud and Holly, found trunks and boxes left over from other presidents. There was a pile of rusted swords and guns in an old wardrobe labeled *Jackson*. We found a minuteman's uniform. It was rotted out along the folds in its cloth. It is from the time of George Washington, says Holly Taft. Mama made us drop the uniform because it had fleas all over it.

We grab Father and get him upstairs to the roof, where we have our fort. There are ten logs all pointed in different directions but mostly to the south. They are our artillery. "These are two-hundred-pounder Parrot siege guns," I tell Father.

"Where'd you find that out?" he asks.

"From the bucktails outside the President's House gates. We talk to them all the time," I say. I

know the bucktails are supposed to be drilling, but they stop and tell us all about army life.

Father strides in and out of our fort with his hands in his pockets. He looks at the southern sky, which is just losing the sun's last light. "Who is that?" asks Father. He points to Jack. Jack is a doll in a Zouave uniform — red pants and a blue tunic. "Why is he hanging by the neck?" asks Father.

Taddie answers. "Jack's a rebel spy," he says. "We have to file charges against him for treason and hang him. Then we bury him in the rose garden. Then we dig him up. The gardener gets mad at us, Papa-day."

Father turns Tad upside down and swings him by his feet. "You must not annoy the gardener, Taddie. He is doing his job, and he doesn't like little boys ruining his roses. You know that. Your mother told you that last week."

"Papa-day, I want a goat, please?" says Taddie.

"Promise not to annoy the gardener?" asks Father.

"Promise!" says Taddie. "When can I have my goat?"

"We will see in the morning," says Father. "In the meantime, boys, I don't think any rebel army is going to come up this way with your seige guns trained right on 'em. No indeed, they won't!"

"You think we'd really scare 'em, Pa?" I ask.

"Scare the pants off 'em!" he says. "Now, come to supper. Mama's waiting."

"Can my goat sleep in the bed with me, Papa-day?" asks Tad.

"He may turn up his nose at your bed and prefer the stables, son," says Father. "We'll have to ask him!"

At supper Mama has covered the dining table with swaths and squares of velvet and silk. Many pieces have gold thread. All are bright colors and soft materials.

"The President's House is not just our house," says Mama. "It's the people's house too. And it is a filthy mess at the moment. We are getting rid of the rotting furniture, the moldy drapes, and the carpets with holes in the middle. Shameful!"

"Mother, don't spend too much of the people's money on the people's house!" says Father, spooning up chicken fricassee. "This is the best place we've ever lived. It's good enough for me without a lot of extra expensive flub-dubs."

"Too many bachelors all in a row!" Taddie and I sing to Pa. That's what Mama says about the house. We know Mama will make the president's mansion beautiful because Mama has top-rail taste, which Father doesn't care about. We also like Mama busy.

"Bachelors!" says Father. "What's bachelors got to do with it?"

"Papa-dear," says Mama. "The last president was a sloppy old bachelor, and the ones before not much better. The one before last let his drooling spaniels up on the furniture. If we don't spruce this old house up, the spiders will take over!"

Later, before bedtime, Taddie asks me, "What is a bachelor?"

"An old man with no wife, no kids, and hair in his nose and ears," I say.

"Just like all those old men in the Cabinet! Just like Governor Chase and Senator Seward and General Scott!" says Taddie.

Governor Chase is the Secretary of the Treasury. Senator Seward is the Secretary of State. We don't like them, Tad and I, because when we come into the Cabinet meetings, they absolutely glare at us as if

their eyes were daggers. Once I heard Mr. Chase say in a loud, huffy whisper to General Scott, "Children should be seen and not heard!" but of course it doesn't matter to Father.

In April, Father tells us that the war has begun somewhere down to South Carolina. Taddie and I make everything ship-shape on the roof in case the rebels want to invade Washington.

Shortly after the war starts, Father goes into a black-dog mood. You can see it on his face. He won't come up for air. One evening I find him staring out a President's House window facing south.

"What are you looking at, Pa?" I want to know.

His hand comes and rests lightly on the top of my head. "See there, to the left of that row of pontoons?" he says, and points to a patch of ground way off in Virginia across the river. "That's land that belongs to Colonel Robert E. Lee and his family."

"Is he the one you want to lead our troops, Pa?"

"He is the best man in the U.S. Army, son. But he is a Virginia man, and Virginia is a slave state. Today Lee took his West Point sword, turned it around handle first, and gave it back. Tears in his eyes, they say. Lee won't serve his country. He's going to bide with the rebels and lead his state against us."

"Don't we have good generals too, Pa?" I ask.

He half closes his left eye and the air comes out of him. "No," he answers so I can hardly hear. "All the clever generals are with the South. We've got the leftovers."

All summer long, Father goes into meetings. This is after he's already seen a hundred people, one after another, in the morning. These meetings are depressing to Father because the war is going so badly for us. The South is winning all the battles.

So oftentimes I say to Tad, "You think he's had enough for the day?"

Tad says, "Yes, let's get 'im!"

So we do. The Cabinet gets really mad, but we don't care. Sometimes we have to throw ourselves on the big Cabinet room table and kick their papers onto the floor. That really steams them up. Father laughs. It is the only time he gets to laugh, he says.

It is Mama's work that goes well. The President's House gains a new carpet as big as the town square in Springfield. It is made of deep wool and dyed with a pattern of ocean waves in blue, green, and white. Tad and Holly and me and Bud love to dive down onto it and pretend to swim. The draper comes and cuts new draperies and re-covers the disgusting sofas, making them beautiful. We boys grab all his discards and make days-of-old robes out of the satin and gold cloth, just as good as the real knights in armor.

Mama is happy with her beautiful new president's mansion. She throws parties and receptions, and she loves dressing up for them. Bob comes down from Harvard for Christmas.

At Christmas Eve supper, Mama says a prayer. We ask God to care for our little brother Eddie in heaven. We thank Him for all His gifts and we ask Him to bless all the souls of the soldiers in the war who have died and help heal the soldiers who are wounded and in pain, on both sides.

As a carol is sung, I see tears brighten in Father's eyes. He holds my hand and Tad's across the table and nods at Bob. "If it were not for my dear codgers here at this table, I could not go on," he says. Mama beams at him down the table. "And your mother," he

adds. "Your precious mother has given me the three best sons in the world."

Tad puts red holly berries in his hair. We are so happy.

Tad

—1862–1865—

Downstairs, the night of the big winter party, a thousand people come to eat and drink and dance in Mama's new and beautiful President's House.

Upstairs, Willie and I lie in our little beds with the fever. We are so sick, we can't sit up to drink water. Mama stays with us. Then Papa-day comes up and makes Mama go downstairs to be nice to the guests. The fevers make me and Willie so weak, says Papa-day, we are like kittens in a hailstorm.

Morning comes, then another night. At last I

open my eyes and the fever has left me. My brother is white as a ghost, wrapped in his blanket, with the doctors around him. Willie does not open his eyes again. Holly Taft comes in to visit us. He holds out his arms. Willie dies inside them. Papa-day hides his face in his hands and falls crossways onto the bed. "Willie is gone to the house of the angels," says Mama when she says anything at all.

Until late spring, Mama stays in bed almost all the time. Her maid, Lizzie Keckley, draws the curtains over the windows because the daylight hurts Mama's eyes. Mama steps out of her bed and goes down crying on the floor. She can't stop. She doesn't even look like Mama when the crying comes over her. She gets all puffy in the face, and her hair streams down on her shoulders. Papa-day tries to calm her, but she twists away, just the same as a dog on the end of a chain. Lizzie washes Mama's face and brushes the tangles out of her hair. To cheer her up, Lizzie brings out one of Mama's special dresses, the prettiest one, but Mama just pushes the dress aside. Some days, first thing in the morning, Lizzie puts Mama back in bed and then they give her laudanum against the crying.

On April 4th, I am nine years old. But Mama will not let Holly and Bud Taft come back to the President's House for my birthday. She says they will never come again because they will remind me of Willie and make me cry. I think it is because they will make Mama cry to see them still alive and well with Willie buried underground, never to be seen again. My crying is done with. It lasted until the end of winter and some of spring.

When Willie was here, he helped me learn my letters because my letters go backward and upside down on the page. Willie did not mind about the upside-down letters. When I said, "Willie, won't you please write my name on the paper for me? Won't you tie my cravat?" he always did.

Now Willie is gone and it is no secret that everyone thinks I am slow because I can't speak crisp the way other boys do. I am not slow. I am just not good at some hard sit-down things. "It's all right, Taddie," Willie always told me. "You're not meant for sit-down work. You're meant to be a soldier." So every day I wear the boy-size uniform that the Secretary of War, Mr. Stanton, gave to me. I feel good-for-something in the uniform, but without Willie, without Bud and Holly, I am very lonely.

Papa-day is lonely too. I heard the servants say that Mama's mourning time should be over and she has gone just sheerly mad. I heard Mr. Nicolay tell that same thing to Mr. Hay. They call Mama "the hell-cat" when they think no one can hear. In church on Sundays I pray she will come out of it.

Papa-day cannot sleep in the bedroom with Mama anymore because she has such nightmares and cries all night long. He sleeps alone in his own bedroom.

"Can I come to bed, Papa-day?" I whisper from his doorway one dark night.

He strikes a match and lights his bedside candle. I see his long arm come out to guide me to the bed. I get under the covers. He sighs a little, but not too sadly.

"Papa-day," I say to him.

"What is it, son?" he asks. He is tired. I hear it.

"Papa-day, I want to go back to Springfield. Can we go back soon?"

He takes a while to answer. "Tadpole, we are stuck in this old house until the war is won and over. Then maybe we'll take a trip home."

"But when will that be, Papa-day?"

He goes away in his sleep. To the land of worry, I think, where I cannot follow.

Even when Mama is able to have supper with us again, there is always the war on Papa-day's mind. When the meal is over, Papa-day marches up and down on the parlor carpet and does what Mama calls "blustering." He smacks the rolled newspaper against his leg and steams off about the man he calls "Little Napoleon." By that he means General McClellan, who's the head of the whole Army of the Potomac. General McClellan should have licked the rebels three times by now, but he has "the slows," says Papa-day.

"Sack him!" says Mama. "Snotty little layabout, defying you, the president. Fire him!"

One evening Papa-day loses his patience entirely. We go over to General McClellan's house on Tenth Street.

"Are you going to fire Little Napoleon tonight, Papa-day?" I ask.

"He won't fire easy, son," says Papa-day. "There's one hundred thousand men in his army. They love him like a daddy. He won't send his army into a fight, though."

"Why won't he fight the war, Papa-day?"

Papa-day says, "I think he's scared of General Lee, waiting in the woods on the other side."

"Are you going to tell him he's a yellow-bellied sapsucker, like Bobby calls him?" I ask.

"Let's just say I want to give him a piece of my mind," is the answer.

After an hour by the hall clock, General McClellan swans in through the front door. He chucks his gloves on the hall table and marches upstairs without so much as a howdy-do to Papa-day, who is, after all, the president of the United States, not to mention commander in chief, waiting in a hard-backed hallway chair. I want to run right upstairs and smack the Little Napoleon, but I am not permitted.

"You stupid Napoleon!" I shout up the stairway after him. "Snotty sapsucker!" but Papa-day's big hand covers my mouth. Laughing, he carries me outside. "That's telling him, son!" he says.

All over the South, thousands of poor soldiers get their legs and arms shot off in different battles. Every night the telegraph office has news of more hundreds killed. Papa-day says he feels the blood of those men wash over him and he can never be clean of it. I think he meshes all those dead boys in the field into his sadness about Willie.

One night we lie in his bed and I have an idea. "Papa-day!" I punch him and wake him up. "Papa-day, if we go home to Springfield, Willie will be there. I know he's there. I know he's in our old house and on our street. Let's go, Papa-day. I promise Willie is there and Bobby will come home from that boring old Harvard and then you and Mama will be happy again."

I wait for him to say something. I wait for that word — *yes!* But it doesn't come. I hear only the night sounds of Washington City. Just a little, the bed trembles. Papa-day is crying quiet as a bird.

For the summer months, we go to a cottage at the Soldiers' Home. It is an hour's ride north of the

President's House. The Soldiers' Home is where old and wounded soldiers are sent. The cottage is a fair-size house, cooler by a mile than the mansion.

Leaving hot old Washington, Mama says we will avoid Potomac fever. Mama worries about fevers all the time. She says the fevers grow in the swamps around Washington. Then the air over the swamps becomes a fever-filled miasma. The miasmas fly through the city in summertime. When it is hot enough, the miasmas come right through the window and make people deathly sick.

In the cottage there are none of those hateful strangers tramping around asking Papa-day for favors every time he pokes his head out of his office. There are no miasmas.

At the cottage, I have my own pony. There are lots of soldiers all around, and I play with them and eat with them and listen when they tell stories.

Mama says to Father, "Tad will learn soldier talk, bad language, from the troops."

Papa-day answers, "Let him heal, Mother. The soldier boys love Tad. They never call him slow or make fun of how he talks." I hear him say that to Mama when they think I am asleep.

Through the summer, Mama still wears black instead of her pretty dresses. On the porch of our cottage, she holds me for long times in her lap. She sways right and left. Sometimes she cries, but it doesn't scare me anymore because it is small crying. We go outside. She walks alongside my pony, her hand on his girth or my stirrup. We go through the meadows and she gets flowers for the dining room.

I wish for the war to be done, so we can go back to Springfield, but it carries on so long I can hardly remember a time before there was a war. With Mama I visit the Washington hospitals. We bring gifts to

the soldiers, who scream and bleed in their cots with their terrible wounds. Some days we bring fruit, other days flowers from the President's House garden. Always we bring a few books to read out loud. Mama writes letters home for the sick soldiers who can't sit up or use their hands.

The war goes through Christmas and then another year and another Christmas. The battles do not go well for us. Papa-day loses weight worrying. Mr. Steinway's nice black suit just hangs on him now. He goes at all hours of the night over to the telegraph office across from the President's House. Lots of times he takes me. Even if it is late at night, he takes me and rides me on his shoulders in my nightshirt. We sit in the little office with the window way up high and listen to the *dit-dit-dot* of the telegraph messages coming in from the commanders. They are fighting the war in Mississippi or in Tennessee or sometimes far, far away in Louisiana.

The telegraph sergeant translates the messages for Papa-day. All those dits and dots mean words. Papa-day answers the messages very carefully. I cannot disturb him while he thinks up his responses, so I am quiet and good.

Papa-day sits in his chair with the squeaky wooden wheels. He rolls back and forth and writes on a pad. He mouths his telegrams aloud just the way he memorizes his works of William Shake-speare, over and over again until he gets it right.

Meanwhile the telegraph sergeant plays card tricks for me and says he'll teach me to be a magician. Papa-day's words are put back into dit-dit-dots on the telegraph key and away they go, back to Tennessee, back to Mississippi, through the air like shooting stars. He calls them lightning messages.

After messages, Papa-day and I walk home to the President's House. "Someday we will win this old war, Papa-day," I tell him. But Mama and I can't get him to eat right now. He pushes his meal away, half-eaten, at suppertime.

"What's happening tomorrow, Papa-day?" I ask one evening.

"Tomorrow I must visit another one of my generals," he answers.

"Can I come?"

"What would I do without you?" asks Papa-day.

I ride my pony and I wear my uniform and I go with him everywhere. Mr. Seward, Mr. Chase, and all the other old men have gotten used to me barging into their Cabinet meetings. They are ho-hum when I bring my goat into the Cabinet room or stand on the big table and show them how I can take my sword out of its scabbard in three seconds flat.

General Scott is gone. Little Napoleon has been fired. Papa-day has a general he likes at last. His name is General Grant. General Grant is good because he brings victories to our side and begins to win the war at last. The bad thing about him is that he kills off thousands more of our soldiers in order to do it. "These terrible deaths are like those of my sons and brothers," says Papa-day. He sleeps less and eats only a green apple for breakfast. I hold his hand at night, and I save my biscuit and milk for him by the bedside in case he wakes up hungry.

On my twelfth birthday, April 4, 1865, Papa-day and I go south from Washington on a steamboat, the *River Queen*. I hear the soldiers talking. They are all excited because at last the war is over and we have won. We are going to visit Richmond, the capital of the rebel South. The South's rebel days are over. They have been smacko-ed but good by General Grant's victorious boys in blue. The military men want a big parade down Richmond's streets, with cannons and band music and American flags to show the rebels who is boss now.

"No," says Papa-day. "We will let them up easy."

In the end it is only Papa-day and me who walk through Richmond under its brown cloud of artillery dust. The houses are crumbled and ruined. Chairs and boxes, chunks of walls and clothing, lie scattered all over the streets. People look at Papa-day's tall hat as we pass under their windows but not a cheer or a happy word comes from them. I hope maybe they will see how brave he is and maybe they will stop being rebels and learn not to hate him so much.

Suddenly we are surrounded by a big crowd of Negro men and women. They are cheering. They

begin to sing hymns and they fall, in tears, at Papa-day's feet. They were all born in slavery but now are free. They thank Papa-day for being the one to free them. They call him Father Abraham and kiss his long legs and feet. Papa-day is embarrassed. "I have freed no one," he says. "All men are born free in the eyes of the Lord. It is the good Lord you must thank."

It is two miles' walk to the rebel president's house. This is the home of the president of the confederate states, Mr. Jefferson Davis. He, who started all this trouble and war, has hightailed it out of Virginia — no one knows where to.

Papa-day and I sit in two comfortable chairs with upholstered footstools in Mr. Davis's front parlor. Papa asks a rebel soldier for a glass of water, and it is brought immediately. We drink the rebel water and we listen to the sound of the now-free slaves singing in their new freedom. "Down by the Riverside" comes out of a hundred mouths. The music of the song floats skyward and joins the brick dust and cannon smoke hanging in the air. Then the old hymn and the war dust sprinkle down together over everything in the city.

When we go home to the President's House the next evening, the whole city of Washington is lit up as if for Christmas. Colored gaslights spell out words that Papa-day reads to me as we pass by. *Peace! Glory to the Union!* say the lights. All of Washington is celebrating our victory.

Papa-day takes me to the upstairs window of the President's House, and I lean out too far. Mr. Nicolay pulls me back in by the seat of my pants. He holds a candle for Papa-day to read a speech. On the President's House lawn, the army band plays "The

Battle Hymn of the Republic" over and over again. It is our Union song. The crowd loves it. When they see Papa-day's face in the candlelight, they quiet on down for him to speak.

I kneel beneath him at his feet and catch the pages of the speech as he drops each one. Little bullets of wax land on my hair from Mr. Nicolay's candle.

Papa-day tells the crowd that there is no room for anger or hatred in our land. When he is finished, the captain signals his band to strike up "Glory, glory, hallelujah" again, but Papa-day shouts down to them to stop. He says, "It's been four years since 'Dixie' has been played in Washington. It may be the rebel hymn, but it's a good old song. Let's have it, Captain!"

The captain conductor hesitates. He doesn't want to play the enemy song for the Union crowd. Papa-day doesn't care. He whispers down to me,

"This crowd wants to rub the South's nose in the mud, but I won't let 'em, Taddie. I won't let 'em."

"Give 'em 'Dixie'!" he orders the band.

The conductor obeys. One by one the people take up the words of the song.

"In Dixie Land where I was born in,
Early on one frosty mornin',
Look away! Look away! Look away! Dixie Land."

We stand at the window and sing with the ocean of people outside. I know better, but still I say, "Papa-day, I know Willie's waiting for us in Springfield. Can we go back home now?"

The word I want comes. "Yes!" he says. "We shall go soon, Tadpole."

I think of all those little towns we must go through again. But at the end will be my brother, his hands full of pebbles. I will kiss him and never pull

his hair again. Mr. Nicolay raises up my hand in the rhythm of the song. I follow Papa-day's eyes. They are trained south, to the Virginia hills that lie in the darkness.

"Do you think they can hear us over there in rebel land, Papa-day?" I ask him. "Can they hear us sing their song?"

"I am sure they can, son," he says. His hand tightens on mine.

Author's Note

The incidents in this story of Abraham Lincoln and his family are grounded in historical fact. No detail was imagined or invented except the dialogue and the circumstances in which it took place. Everything I have written was easily researched because Lincoln's life may be more thoroughly documented than any other person's in history.

The first year the Lincoln family spent in the President's House was preserved by Bud and Holly's sister, Julia Taft Bayne, who later wrote about it in a splendid short book, *Tad Lincoln's Father* (Little, Brown, 1931). Elizabeth Keckley also wrote about the Lincoln family, as did many of the president's colleagues, friends, and military staff who came and went in the family's life in Washington during the war. Their recollections are collected in a book called *Lincoln As I Knew Him*, edited by Harold Holzer (Algonquin, 1999). It was in that book, while doing research for a historical novel about the Civil War, that I first came across the two-hundred-word fragment by Willie Lincoln about a trip taken with his father. That was the beginning of *Lincoln and His Boys*.

Throughout my reading, I marveled at how kind Lincoln was with his sons. His boys could do no wrong. Willie and Tad Lincoln were raised to have fun in the Victorian era, when fun in public, especially for children, was frowned upon. Lincoln's law partner and later his Cabinet members disapproved of the boys' wild behavior. Lincoln didn't give a hoot what they thought.

Abraham Lincoln lived a remarkable life. It has been my greatest joy to read deeply in the nooks and crannies of it. Folded into the Lincoln history of political and military genius, of brilliant writing and public speaking, of mental illness, poverty, murder, and national sainthood, is the portrait of a generous and patient father, far ahead of his time.